A DK PUBLISHING BOOK

Managing Editor Bridget Gibbs
Editor Fiona Munro
US Editor Kristin Ward
Designer Lisa Hollis
Photography Steve Gorton
DTP Designer Kim Browne
Production Katy Holmes

Rhymes selected by Shona McKellar

First American Edition, 1998
2 4 6 8 10 9 7 5 3 1
Published in the United States by DK Publishing, Inc.,
95 Madison Avenue, New York, New York 10016

Visit us on the World Wide Web at http://www.dk.com

A catalog record is available from the Library of Congress.

ISBN 0-7894-2861-X

Color reproduction by Colourscan, Singapore.
Printed in Singapore.

DK would like to thank the following for appearing in this book:
Jake George-Samuels, Rebekah Murrell, Sarah and Harry Hayden,
Merryl, Phoebe, and Martha Epstein, Hideyuki and Amané Sobue, Freya Hartas,
Alison and Harriet Hunter, Neeraj and Naveena Kapur, Bindi Haria, Sally and Jake Davies,
Alex Squire Melmoth, Shanti Gorton, Raphael Cox, Caitlin and Madeleine Hennessy.

Playtime
Rhymes

Illustrated by Priscilla Lamont

DK PUBLISHING, INC.

Contents

Knock at the Door

Knock on forehead

Knock at
the door,

Lift eyebrow

Peep in,

Push nose up

Lift the latch,

Ring the bell,

Put finger in mouth

And walk in.

I Saw a Slippery, Slithery Snake

I saw a slippery, slithery snake

Slide through the grasses, making them shake.

Weave hands from side to side

Circle eyes

He looked at me with his beady eye.

"Go away from my pretty, green garden," said I.

Go away!

"Hiss," said the slippery, slithery snake

Repeat first action

As he slid through the grasses, making them shake.

9

Round and Round the Garden

Round and round the garden,

Went the teddy bear.

One step, two steps,

Tickly under there.

Round and round the haystack,

Went the little mouse.

One step, two steps,

To his little house.

Circle palm

Walk fingers up…

baby's arm…

tickle!

Slowly, Slowly

Slowly, slowly, very slowly
Creeps the garden snail.
Slowly, slowly, very slowly
Up the wooden rail.

tummy

baby's...

slowly up...

Walk hand...

Quickly, quickly, very quickly
Runs the little mouse.
Quickly, quickly, very quickly
All around the house.

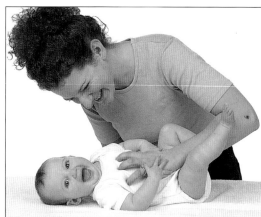

Tickle baby throughout second verse

This Little Pig Went to Market

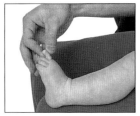

Wiggle…

This little pig
went to market.

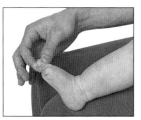

each…

This little pig
stayed at home.

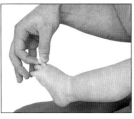

toe…

This little pig
had roast beef.

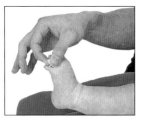

in…

This little pig
had none.

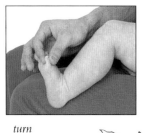

turn

And this little
pig cried…

Wee-wee-wee

Tickle!

all the way home.

12

These are Grandma's Glasses

These are Grandma's glasses,

This is Grandma's hat;

Grandma claps her hands like this,

And rests them in her lap.

These are Grandpa's glasses,

This is Grandpa's hat;

Grandpa folds his arms like this,

And takes a little nap.

Seesaw, Margery Daw

Rock backward and forward

Seesaw, Margery Daw,

Johnny shall have a new master,

He shall have but a penny a day,

Because he can't work any faster.

Seesaw, Jack sat down.

Which is the way to Boston Town?

One foot up, and the other foot down,

That is the way to Boston Town.

Here's a Ball for Baby

Here's a ball for baby,
Big and fat and round.

Here is baby's hammer,
See how it can pound.

Here are baby's soldiers,
Standing in a row.

Here is baby's music,
Clapping, clapping so.

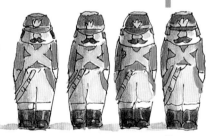

Pudding on the Plate

Rock from side to side

Pudding on the plate,

Pudding on the plate,

Wibble wobble,

Wibble wobble,

Pudding on the plate.

Candies in the jar,

Candies in the jar,

Shake them up,

Shake them up,

Candies in the jar.

Bounce up and down

Blow!

Candles on the cake,

Candles on the cake,

Blow them out,

Blow them out,

Puff, puff, puff!

Itsy-bitsy Spider

The itsy-bitsy spider
    climbed up the water spout,

*Touch index fingers and thumbs
in turn by twisting wrists*

Down came the rain
    and washed the spider out.

*Raise hands and wiggle fingers as
you lower*

Out came the sun
    and dried up all the rain,

*Raise hands and make a wide
circle with arms*

Then the itsy-bitsy spider
    climbed up the spout again.

Repeat first action

17

Two Little Dicky Birds

Two little dicky birds
Sitting on a wall,

One named Peter,
One named Paul.

Fly away, Peter!
Fly away, Paul!

Come back, Peter,
Come back, Paul.

There's a Wide-Eyed Owl

There's a wide-eyed owl
With a pointed nose,
He has pointed ears
And claws for toes.
He sits in a tree
And looks at you,
Then flaps his wings and says,

"Who...who...whooo!"

Five Little Peas

Five little peas in a peapod pressed,

One grew, two grew, and so did all the rest.

They grew…and grew…and did not stop,

Until one day the pod went…POP!

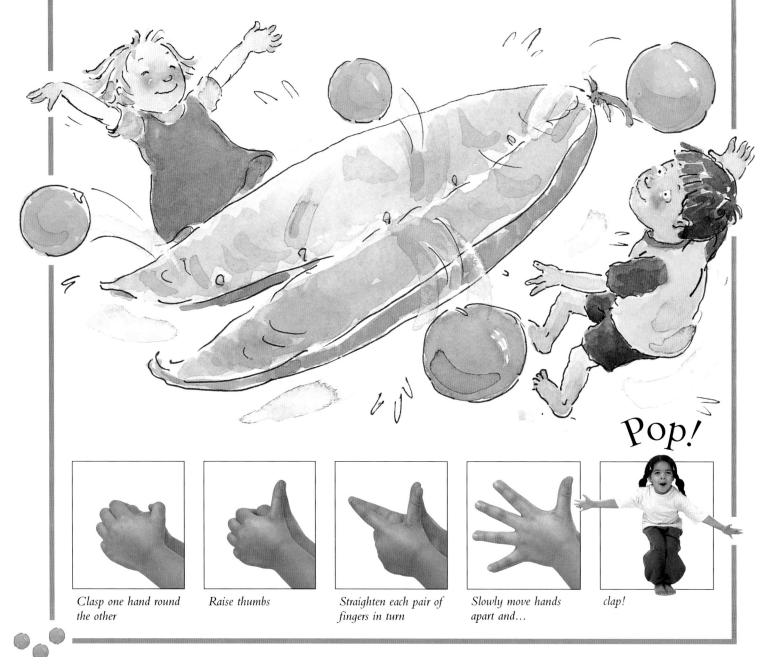

Pop!

Clasp one hand round the other

Raise thumbs

Straighten each pair of fingers in turn

Slowly move hands apart and…

clap!

20

Cobbler, Cobbler

Cobbler, cobbler, fix my shoe,

Get it done by half-past two,

Now my toe is peeping through,

Cobbler, cobbler, mend my shoe.

Bang fists together

Poke index finger through fingers of other hand

Repeat first action

21

What Do You Suppose?

What do you suppose?
A bee sat on my nose!

Then what do you think?
He gave me a wink,

And said, "I beg your pardon,
I thought you were the garden!"

Fly away, bee!

Pat-a-cake

Pat-a-cake, pat-a-cake, baker's man,

Bake me a cake as fast as you can.

Pat it and prick it and mark it with B,

And put it in the oven

　　for Baby and me.

Clap in rhythm

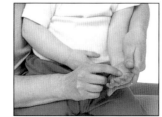
"Pat" and "prick" baby's hand

Trace "B"

Slide cake into oven

Two Little Men in a Flying Saucer

Two little men in a flying saucer

Flew around the world one day.

Move baby's arms up and down

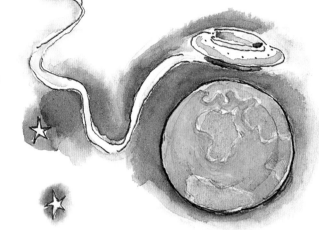

Lift baby and move in a circle

They looked to the left and

right a bit,

Turn head to left and right

And couldn't bear the sight of it,

And then they flew away.

Cover eyes

Repeat first action

24

This is the Way the Ladies Ride

*Bounce baby, getting faster as rhyme progresses,
and lowering baby between knees at end*

This is the way the ladies ride,
Nimble-nim, nimble-nim.

This is the way the gentlemen ride,
Gallop-a-trot, gallop-a-trot.

This is the way the farmers ride,
Jiggety-jog, jiggety-jog.

This is the way the delivery boy rides,
Tripperty-trot, tripperty-trot,

Till he falls in a ditch with a flipperty,
Flipperty, flop, flop, FLOP!

Build a House with Five Bricks

Build a house with five bricks,
One, two, three, four, five.

Place fists on top of each other in turn

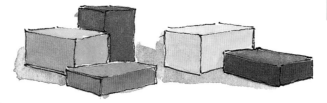

Make a roof

Put a roof on top

And a chimney, too

Straighten arms for chimney

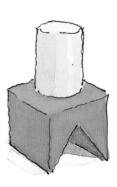

Blow!

Where the wind blows through!

whoo whoo

Here is the Church

Here is
the church,

Interlace fingers

Here is the steeple,

Point index fingers

Open the doors,

Open thumbs

And here are the people.

Turn hands over and wiggle fingertips

Here is the minister
going upstairs,

Walk fingers of one hand up fingers of other hand

And here he is
a-saying his prayers.

Pray

27

Hickory Dickory Dock

Clap three times

Hickory dickory dock,

Walk fingers up arm

The mouse
ran up the clock.

Clap once

The clock
struck one,

Walk fingers down arm

The mouse
ran down,

Clap three times

Hickory dickory dock.

The Baby in the Cradle

The baby in the cradle
Goes rock-a-rock-a-rock.

The clock on the dresser
Goes tick-a-tick-a-tock.

The rain on the window
Goes tap-a-tap-a-tap,

But here comes the sun,
So we clap-a-clap-a-clap!

Rock arms   *Swing arm from side to side*   *Tap finger on hand*   *Clap three times*